Published by Scholastic Inc.
90 Old Sherman Turnpike, Danbury, Connecticut 06816.

For information regarding permission, write to:
Disney Licensed Publishing
114 Fifth Avenue, New York, New York 10011.

ISBN 0-7172-8722-X

Designed and produced by Bill SMITH STUDIO.

Printed in the U.S.A.
First printing, September 2002

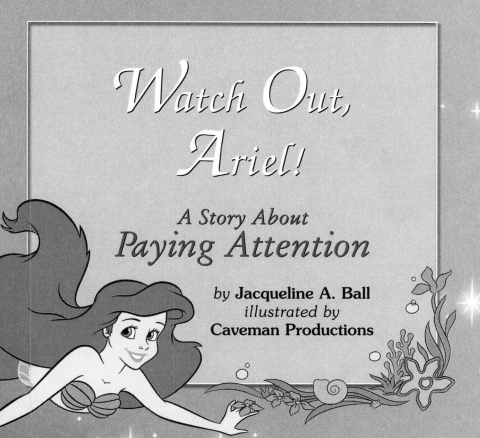

Watch Out, Ariel!

A Story About
Paying Attention

by **Jacqueline A. Ball**
illustrated by
Caveman Productions

SCHOLASTIC INC.

New York   Toronto   London   Auckland   Sydney
Mexico City   New Delhi   Hong Kong   Buenos Aires

King Triton had summoned his seven daughters to the throne room. Sebastian the crab was already there.

"*O*ur new royal ballroom is finished," Triton told them. "There will be a celebration party tonight, and I have a special job for each of you."

Triton turned to Sebastian. "I want you to compose some new music."

"Yes, Your Majesty," said Sebastian proudly.

"Arista," Triton continued, "I'm putting you in charge of the food. Alana, you'll be responsible for the invitations. Aquata . . ."

The Princesses listened—all except Ariel.

Ariel was daydreaming about the kinds of parties humans had. Scuttle the sea gull had told her they did something called *dancing*.

$\mathcal{D}$ancing! What would it be like to spin around on legs? Ariel imagined herself twirling around and around and—

"Ariel," Triton said sharply. "Are you listening to me?"

Ariel snapped out of her daydream. "Sorry, Daddy. Could you please say that again?"

Triton sighed. "I want you to gather plants to decorate the ballroom."

"Of course, Daddy," Ariel said. Happily, she scooped up the shells for the necklace she was making. Then she headed to the ballroom to see how many plants she would need.

"*O*h, Arrrielll," Sebastian called. He pointed to her bag. "I was wondering if I could use some of your shells to make special music for the party."

But Ariel wasn't listening. "Do you know where I can find lots of pretty plants?" she asked instead.

"Out past the giant clamshell," the crab replied. "Near three red rocks and two blue coral pieces. But Ariel, about those shells—"

"Thanks," Ariel called, swimming away.

Ariel swam into the ballroom. An octopus was wrapping strands of pearls around giant green columns.

"*T*hose pearls will help, but it will take lots of plants to dress up this room," she thought. She imagined how beautiful the room would look.

*T*hen she imagined herself at the party. She spun around in the water, tapping her tail in time to imaginary music.

"Watch out, Princess Ariel!" cried the octopus. But Ariel twirled right into him. Pearls floated off in every direction.

"Oh, I'm sorry!" Ariel cried. "I wasn't paying attention. Let me help."

When all the pearls were picked up, Ariel
swam out and found her friend Flounder.
Quickly they swam to the giant clamshell.
"Now where, Ariel?" asked Flounder.
But Ariel couldn't remember.

She scratched her head. "It's near two blue rocks, or was it three red coral pieces?" Ariel sighed. "I wish I had been paying better attention when Sebastian gave me directions."

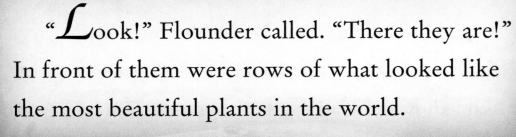

"*L*ook!" Flounder called. "There they are!"
In front of them were rows of what looked like
the most beautiful plants in the world.

Ariel swam between the rows. "Let's start picking them, Flounder."

Suddenly a small, but angry, voice cried out, "Come any closer and I'll sting!"

Ariel and Flounder backed away in alarm.
"We're not flowers. We're animals!" shouted
the little voice.

"Flounder! It's a sea anemone," Ariel
whispered. "They're as beautiful as flowers. But
those 'petals' are really tentacles that can sting."

"We won't hurt you," Ariel told the anemone. "We just need some pretty plants for a party. Do you know where I can find any?"

"No. I never go anywhere. But I wish *I* could go to a party," the anemone said.

Around him, other anemones waved and bobbed their tentacles in agreement.

Ariel couldn't imagine being stuck in one place. She also understood how the anemones felt—Ariel wished *she* could go to a human party one day.

*A*riel and Flounder waved good-bye to the anemones and swam away. Eventually, they found the place Sebastian had described.

"Hooray!" said Ariel. "I'd better get to work."

Soon she had a huge pile of plants.

Her mind wandered as she bent down to pick one more. But it wasn't a plant at all. It was the tentacle of a sleeping squid!

"Ariel! Look out!" cried Flounder.

Too late! The angry squid shot out a cloud of black ink that covered Ariel and all her pretty plants.

"Oh, no!" cried Ariel. "They're ruined! This is all my fault," she said to herself. "I should have been paying attention."

$\mathcal{N}$ow the ballroom would never be decorated. Worse, as Ariel thought about her day, she realized she had disappointed others.

What would a princess do?

$\mathcal{A}$riel decided she would pay attention—starting now.

Remembering what the anemone had said, she and Flounder went back and asked him to the ball.

"Oh, yes," the anemone said eagerly. "But could all my brothers and sisters come, too?"

Ariel thought about it. Soon she had a plan.

That night at the ball, Ariel twirled and whirled as Sebastian played his new song.

"*T*hank you for the seashells, Ariel," Sebastian sang. "Filling these shells with pearls makes such wonderful music!"

riel smiled. She waved at her friend, the yellow anemone.

"This is great!" he called. "Thanks for bringing us all to the party."

"You're welcome!" Ariel replied.

*T*hen Triton gave Ariel a big hug and said, "The ballroom looks beautiful. Better still, you've made some fellow sea creatures happy."

Ariel smiled. "It wasn't very hard when I really paid attention."

The End